BEATEN

HEART

The Forever Love Collection #2

This Book
Belongs
To
Katie

HAZEL ROBINSON

DEDICATION

THIS THANK YOU IS NOT TO ONE OR TWO PEOPLE,
ITS TO EVERY SINGLE PERSON THAT CAN, RELATE,
SYMPATHISE OR GROW STRENGTH FROM
MANDY'S STORY.

People say getting out is the hardest part, but they are wrong, they have no idea. The hardest part is getting out and staying out, it's adjusting your life to a whole new way, it's healing wounds that they can't see, it's learning to be strong. It's learning to trust and love again.

CHAPTER ONE

You want me, you need me, and you never want to lose me.

I make my escape across the hall and down the stairs, taking one last look at the place I once called home. Every inch of this house belongs to me; the painting above the fire, the table and chairs. I built this home with every inch of my heart, and he shattered it all.

I dig every bit of strength I have inside me, stopping at the front door. My hand runs over the table which stands at the entryway, where each evening the sound of his keys landing on the table would instantly send a shudder to my gut, not knowing which part of him would appear in the kitchen behind me. My heart would race, blood pumping through my veins while the excitement and worry fought against each other.

Some days his tender hand would curl around my waist, spinning me into his loving arms, embracing me with a longing kiss. Other times, I would cower under his hand, or his cruel words would poison my ears.

We met in high school. I fell hard and fast for him, then my world crashed down around me. I lost my mother... He was my rock. I changed; became dependent on him, I needed his love. I needed him to help me heal, and he did. Once I turned eighteen, we married. I went from teenager to housewife all in one day.

I lost all contact with my father after marrying Thomas. He thought the only reason Thomas married me was because I'd inherit the money my mother left for me. My father tried so hard to warn me, but I wouldn't listen, if *only* I had listened.

"Come on, Miranda! You need to get out of here before he wakes up!" My best friend, Hayley, hushes me out the door. She'd once been new, nosy neighbor, but as Thomas' aggression grew, so did our friendship. Three weeks ago I decided to leave him, and she put all the plans into place for me.

"Start the car, Hayley. I'm ready." I climb in the car next to her, closing my eyes to the life I knew, and drift into sleep.

After travelling for over six hours we arrive at my new hideout; a small, two-bedroom cottage deep in the hills of Cumbria. Hayley made all the arrangements and purchasing, now nothing can be traced back to me. I can't risk any evidence being found of my plans. Thomas controls all the banks except one – the one my mother set up for me which contains my inheritance. I contacted the bank several days before, had it shut down, and transferred all funds into a new secret account.

There is no way he can get his hands on my money now.

Standing at the white panel gate, I take a deep sigh of relief.

"Isn't it perfect?" she whispers in my ear.

"Miss Hart?" A man pulls the gate open and offers a firm handshake. "I'm Peter, the estate agent. Shall we go inside?"

***

Thirty minutes later, Peter leaves the cottage, and Hayley and I are left alone. The open-plan downstairs living area hosts a beautiful, log-burning fire and wooden floors, just like the kind of cottage you dream about escaping to on holiday; a romantic cottage in a secluded place, perfect for someone who doesn't want to be found.

I sigh a little at the thought of what I've left behind. This is the first time I actually went through with leaving him. My last attempt to run away didn't go so well, he caught me at the train station, and when he took me home I'd been made to feel ashamed for walking out on my doting husband; if only people knew what he's really like. This time I've covered my tracks.

Sadness bellows through my veins at the comment my mother used to say. *'Love is like a butterfly; you have to be gentle with it or it will perish.'* If only Thomas had listened to the words as much as I.

Standing in the archway between the kitchen and living area, I cross my arms over my middle. "He's going to know you helped me, Hayley." I turn to her, a tear trickles down my cheek.

"Listen to me, Miranda. Don't worry about him. There is no chance he's going to find you all the way out here."

When I feel her arms lock around my neck I almost burst into tears, but I hold them back. I promised myself there will be no more tears; not now that I am free.

"I really should leave, I'll try and get back to see you as soon as I can, but for now, remember, no contact at all. I'm so sorry I have to leave you here alone. Are you going to be okay?"

"I'm sure! I'll be just fine here." I give her one

last hug and watch her leave.

Am I? Will I be okay? Standing at the door with a cup in my hand, the realization of my new life hits me. Alone in the beautiful open country with nothing but hills and trees.

CHAPTER TWO

Love, honor and obey! You made me do all three.

"Thomas, no! Please don't. It hurts...." I jump up from the chair, my heart pounds hard against my chest. I must have fallen asleep. Checking the window, I realize it's dark. I look over to the clock – 10pm.

I have been trapped in this little cottage for three days, and each night the dreams hurt more than the reality. I make my way up the stairs, hoping a soak in the bath will soothe me. I stare at myself in the mirror, the bruises on my arms are fading away. I can handle the pain from his hands, but what hurts the most are the words he speaks, each time ripping deeper and deeper into my skin. He's made me worthless and empty from the inside out. Grinding me down piece by piece, it's his way of controlling me without leaving marks;

these scars are invisible, they are the ones that won't ever fade or heal...they will stay with me forever.

After a long hot bath, I pull my tangled blonde curls into a bun and crawl into bed, my eyes falling heavy.

A loud bang snaps me awake. Shooting up in the bed, I clutch the duvet cover around me as a cold breeze sweeps in from the open window. Tiptoeing across the cold wooden floor, I pull the window shut and examine from where the loud bang had come. A sigh of relief escapes my lungs when I realize the garden gate isn't locked, and is slamming open and shut in the wind.

'Now I'm really wide awake!' I think to myself, grabbing the throw off the bed I creep downstairs to make a cup of my lemon tea. I sit in the armchair looking out the window, pull out my notepad, and start making lists of what I need to do.

How do I divorce him without him knowing where I am? And I really need to make a trip into town tomorrow and pick up a few bits — I only managed to pack a few clothes before leaving.

Just as I'm about to turn the light off and go back to bed, I hear a scratching sound from outside and a whimper. Peering through the glass at the front door I can't see anything, but the whimper grows louder. Taking a brave, deep breath, I open the door and my blood runs cold. "Oh! You poor baby." I bend down to the large German Sheppard laying hurt on my porch, its leg is bleeding. Cautiously, reaching out to stroke it, I examine the dog closer. "No collar huh... Who would keep you out at this time?" The dog stands up on wobbly legs and follows me into the house.

I lay a blanket on the floor and turn on the fire, getting some water and a bandage before guiding the dog onto the fabric. "Now then, let's clean you up," I whisper, stroking over the dog's belly with one hand whilst the other presses a wet cloth over the wound. He lets out a whimper, but soon calms as I wash away the blood. Happy the wound is fully clean, I wrap the bandage around it and fetch the dog a small bowl of water for the night. "You rest here, and tomorrow I'll find your owner."

Tucking myself back down under the duvet, I can't help but worry about my new companion lying down stairs on his own.

***

Early the next morning with the sun glaring through my window, I jump out of bed and head downstairs, finding the dog still fast asleep on the blanket. Creeping in the kitchen I put the kettle on the stove, and whilst rummaging in the fridge for something I can feed him, I hear its paws tapping on the kitchen floor. "What's up, boy? Do you need to go out?" Stroking over his head, I lead him to the back door and let him outside. Once out he rushes off down the path, his leg clearly feeling better. I leave the door open and step back in the house.

As I go to get dressed, he sits at the bottom of the stairs, waiting for me to come back down.

"Right. Come on, boy, let's see if we can find your owner." I tap the side of my leg for him to follow out the door.

The lane I live on consists of five cottages scattered along a never-ending winding road, and I have to walk to the bottom of the lane to catch the bus into the village. I don't care, it's just the way I want it. After knocking on a couple of the houses and getting nowhere with my dog-owner questions, I reach the last house on the lane. The first thing I notice is how beautiful the garden to the property is. Magnificent flowers in all shades of yellow and orange grow on either side of the path. I take a deep breath, flooding my nostrils with the sweet scent and tap on the door.

Nervously stroking the dog's head, I wait as the door begins to open. "Hello," I hear the husky voice. "Can I help you?" As the door opens fully I can see the face behind the voice, standing with his arms crossed over his chest, firm and attentive.

"Hello, I'm Mandy," holding my shaky hand out I wait for a response, I'd been taught to be polite, but the thought of a man touching me in any kind of way sends a shiver of fear down my spine.

Leaving Thomas is just the beginning of my journey to healing, I can't trust another won't be the same; I can't trust another won't be just as painful as the last.

Still standing stern, he stares into my eyes, and something inside me is screaming to get out. "I'm Billy, how can I help you, Mandy?"

As his hand touches mine I have a strange felling deep in the pit of my stomach, like something has awakened, it's like an instant knee-jerk reaction. My mind screams caution, but my body burst to life. "I, I just moved onto the lane a couple of days ago, and well, late last night I found this lonely boy lying on my step," the dog moves close, sitting by my side. "I'm just trying to find his owner."

"I'm sorry, I can't help you, I haven't seen

anyone around here with him." He steps out and kneels in front of the dog. "He is a beautiful dog though. Such a shame." He stands for a second, smiling at the dog. "Would you like to come in for a cup of tea?"

"That would be lovely, thank you." I feel uneasy and out of my depth with him, but his smile, instantly intoxicating, is pulling me in.

"Well, it's nice to finally see someone living in the Moors house, such a shame seeing that lovely house empty for so long." I sit watching him moving around his kitchen.

"Did you know them well?" I curl my cold hands around the hot mug.

Turning to me, he throws the tea-towel on the counter, smiling. "Yes, they lived there for as long as I can remember, lovely old couple –until Mr Moors died, I don't think Elinor could stand living there without him anymore. One day she just caught the bus to town and never came back. My grandfather told me they moved into that house when they were eighteen years old, he carried her over the threshold every year on their anniversary!"

My heart cried. "That's such a sad, beautiful story, did they not have any children?"

"No, just the two of them." He sat at the table next to me.

"I love the house, it's beautiful." I shifted my chair back a little, giving me room to get up. "I really must be getting back, thank you for the tea."

He stands up, holding out his hand. "It was nice to meet you, Mandy." I hesitate at his gesture, before reaching and taking hold of his hand.

"Me too, and thank you." I smile and walk away. "Come on, boy, you can stay with me until someone claims you."

***

I sit on the sofa curled up in front of the fire with the dog sitting right beside me. All the time we are together he never leaves my side. "Maybe I should give you a name until we find your owner, what do you think?" The dog rolls his eyes up to look at me before closing them shut again. I kneel on the floor examining him. "What about Beast? You sure gave me a fright last night, and I don't think anyone will come snooping round here with a big dog like you." Happy with the name, he rolls over, wanting me to rub his belly. "Beast it is then, although I don't really think you're much of a Beast with this hanging out all over." I giggle while tugging on his belly.

***

I replay my meeting with Billy over and over in my head as I lay in bed wide awake. When you've loved someone for so long, you forget how to function without them; Thomas has that hold over me, but for the briefest moment I think I can move on from him.

I could... why shouldn't I?

I spent my whole adult life living in the shadow of someone else, and now I don't know who I am or what I am meant to do. I can function independently as a person, but what about as a woman? Do I live the rest of my life alone, living in fear of love?

Do I not deserve to be loved?

CHAPTER THREE

A man's touch is a precious thing. A monster's touch is a haunting memory.

I gather up my handbag and leave Beast asleep on the chair while I take a trip into town. I sit at a table in the café and ponder over the last few days of my life. I've hid my secret well from Thomas. He had no idea I planned to leave him. The last time he hit me he promised that was it, but I knew it wouldn't be, it never was. There's always a next time where I've done something to *'push'* him to it. Always my fault, but now he will never be able to find or hurt me again.

Walking from shop to shop with hands full of goodies for Beast, I pass a hardware store with a handyman service. I pause for a moment, knowing I have a few jobs that need doing around the house. Breathing deep I push the door open with my back, and approach the tall, slender woman at the counter. "Hello, my name is Mandy. I'm looking for a handyman."

"Billy! Someone here to see you!" the woman shouts down one of the aisles. "Boss won't be a minute," she gives me a smile and carries on filing her nails.

'Billy', I remember the name from the other day with Beast, *'it can't be the same Billy, can it?'* Butterflies start in my stomach as I stand waiting for the man to come down the aisle. As he walks past me and goes behind the counter my heart beats so fast I think I'm going to pass out. "You know, Annie, there are more important things to do in the store than filing your nails! I need all this stuff loaded in my truck please." He passes the piece of paper to the sulky looking woman.

"Okay, back to business. How can I help you?" His eyes shift from the computer screen to me, and he smiles when he realizes who I am. "Oh! Hey, Mandy, isn't it? We have to stop meeting like this.

How can I help you this time?"

"I'm looking for a handyman, there are a few jobs around the cottage that need doing." My hands begin to sweat, and I can feel my cheeks getting redder and redder.

Billy checks the clock behind him before turning his deep green eyes back to me; eyes that just shatter my nerves into tiny pieces. Why do I feel like this around him? "That's something I can help you with, do you mind just waiting in my office through that door while I lock the front door? It's closing time." Billy guides me to the door and leaves me sitting at his desk.

I sit twiddling my fingers together while waiting for him to return, my nerves begin to eat away at me, and I am hungry. I try to remember if I ate, but I can't. The door shuts loudly, making me jump in my seat.

"Sorry about that. Now, where were we?" Billy strides around the table, taking the seat opposite me. Something about the way he holds himself, firm and assertive, makes me curious. "So what kind jobs need sorting out?" He leans forward, resting his elbows on the desk.

I can't help but breathe in his scent, his aftershave over-taking me. Quickly shaking myself out of the thought, I notice him sitting, waiting for my response. "Sorry." I shake myself out of the trance he holds. "The gate doesn't shut or lock properly, there is a leak from the bathroom sink, and two of the kitchen cupboard doors don't shut correctly either I know this sounds silly, but I really need some shelfs putting up."

Smiling, Billy sits back in the chair, resting his hands on his head. "Not silly at all, Mandy. I can come and have a look at the jobs if you would like? And if you think of anything else that needs doing, just let me know."

"Great, when could you come and have a look?" I question.

"I can nip in tomorrow if you're not busy? I'm juggling my time now; my sister is getting ready to leave for college, and I'm in the middle of looking for someone else to cover the shifts she normally works." Billy takes hold of a picture on his desk and passes it over to me. "This is my sister, as much of a pain in the ass as she is I'm going to miss her when she leaves, and this place is going to take it hard too. She's been working around here since she was twelve."

"So, is this a family business then?" I watch him put the picture back on his desk.

"You can say that. My grandad opened this place fifty years ago. My dad didn't want to work here when my grandad died so I took over, and I've been here since. We've extended the store since I took over, and I started the handyman service. So yeah, it's pretty much my life right now." Billy laughs loudly.

"That's great that you took over from your grandfather, I bet he'd be very proud of you." I smile at him.

"Yeah, I like to think so." Billy winks as he

stands up.

I nod as he walks around the desk, picking up my bags. "Come on, I'll give you a ride home, you don't want to be carrying all these bags down that lane." He opens the door, signaling me to walk in front of him. "Oh, I forgot to ask, did you have any luck finding the dog's owner?"

I turn to answer him, catching him watching me walk, and my cheeks redden again. "No, he's still at my place for the moment. I thought about putting some posters up, but I don't have a computer or anything."

Billy puts all my bags in the back of his truck and opens the passenger door for me. "I can help with that, if you want?"

"Do you mind?" I ask as he climbs in the driver seat and starts the engine.

"Of course not, leave it to me."

***

After Billy drops me off at home, I unpack all the shopping, and wander around the house, looking for any other jobs Billy could sort out for me. If I'm completely honest with myself, he makes me quite uncomfortable. He's too sure of himself for me to relax around him, yet on the other hand he's been very friendly towards me.

Snapping out of my thoughts, I finish washing the dishes and go off to run a bath, leaving Beast downstairs on his new bed I bought him.

Sitting in the bath, I reluctantly let thoughts of Thomas enter my mind. I remember the very first time he hit me. It was around the time of our first wedding anniversary, and my nineteenth birthday. We planned a big celebration with all our friends and family, but I'd forgotten to pick his suit up, and ended up being hit right across the face. Of course, he was apologetic and blaming it on me.

Yanking the towel off the rail, I fill with anger at the thought of his hand on me. The last three years were the worst. It became a regular event to have his rage taken out on me when I failed to follow his orders.

Sliding down the bathroom door, I sit on the floor as trickles of tears fall for the forgotten memory of what I almost had. There was a time we were happy before he put the ring on my finger, we were in love a long time ago. I remember the butterflies in my stomach each time he touched me, I remember how tender he kissed me. We had so many dreams and hopes for our future.

I didn't just lose myself being with Thomas, I lost my family, my dignity and my self-worth. Now that I'm free, will I ever get any of it back?

CHAPTER FOUR

It's not just the house that needs fixing.

Sitting in my garden with a cup of tea in my hand, I'm both excited and nervous about Billy coming by this morning. It's why I've been awake for most of the night, tossing and turning, unable to get his face out of my mind.

"Why am I so hung up over this guy?" I really wish I could answer my own question, but a loud knock on the door shakes me from my thoughts. Rushing through the house, I check my reflection in the mirror before swinging the door open.

"Hey!" I come across a little excited.

"Morning." Billy stands with a notebook and tool bag in his hand. Butterflies dance around my chest, watching him stroll into my house wearing a thin white t-shirt and jeans. I hadn't realized how dark his blue eyes are, but standing so close to him, I'm lost in their hypnotizing trance.

Billy clears his throat.

"Sorry." I jump from my stupid gawking at him. "Would you like a cup of tea?"

Smiling, he nods.

Shit. Can I make it any more obvious? Typical desperate housewife move, getting the handyman over. Rushing into the kitchen I make him a cup of tea, and make my way back into the living room.

"Here you go." I pass him the cup.

"Okay, what is it you want me to look at?" He places his cup on the coffee table.

"The tap upstairs in the bathroom is leaking, the gate... and here, I'll show you the cupboard doors in the kitchen." I walk into the kitchen with Billy following behind.

Placing his bag on the table, he examines the two doors that are hanging off, pulling a screwdriver from his tool kit, he quickly fixes them. "That's one job sorted. Bathroom?"

"Top of the stairs, take a left and it's the last door on the landing." When he walks by and makes his way up the stairs, I sigh in relief. Left alone, I regain my composure. Heading to the back door for some fresh air, I can hear him whistling in the bathroom.

After a few minutes he appears behind me. "Bad news is the tap is knackered, you could really do with a new one, but the good news is I've fixed it for the time being. I'll have to nip back with a new one at some point."

"That's fine." I take a sip of my tea.

"And the gate could really do with replacing too, it's falling apart." He pulls the notebook from his back pocket. "So, if you want I'll book you in for Tuesday. I'll sort the tap, put the shelving up, and get the new gate sorted, I've already got the measurements." He brushes his fingers through his hair, staring at me.

"That's great, thank you," I nervously twiddle with the hem of my shirt.

"I really should get going, I've got a garden to

sort this morning too." Packing his bag back up his face tells a different story.

"Do you really have to shoot off? You haven't finished your tea." I don't know why I want him to stay.

Winking at me, he places his bag back on the table and picks up his cup. "Well, maybe I could stay a bit longer, if you want?"

"I don't want to put you out or anything, I mean, if you have somewhere you should be, don't let me stop you." I walk back out to the garden, taking a seat at the table. Billy sits next to me.

"You have a very overgrown garden, Mandy!" He looks down the long garden.

I can't help but laugh at the understatement. "Yes, I haven't really had time to come out here yet and sort it." The grass is taller than Beast in some places, and it's hard to tell which are weeds and which are flowers.

"Do you want me to sort it for you? It won't take me long."

"No, it's fine, I love gardening... It's about the only thing I was able to do at my old place. I'll be fine sorting it on my own, thanks." The reality is that was the only thing I loved doing back home, tending the garden. It's as far out from the house as I was allowed to be without him.

Sitting in the garden on sunny days became my escape from the walls that haunted me. I had a summer house built at the bottom of the garden, next to the rose bushes I watched bloom year after year. I loved it there, reading, relishing the flowers' fragrant scent.

I must have fallen silent for too long, I hadn't noticed Billy already finished his tea, staring at me from across the table. "Are you okay, Mandy?"

"I'm fine." I pull myself back to reality. "Just drifting off, thinking about what to do with the garden." I smile at him.

"Well, I really should get going now. This garden isn't going to sort itself." He stands, stretching his arms out. "If you need anything else, let me know, it's not like I live far away!" he laughs, heading into the house.

'I have a lot more that needs fixing, I'm just not ready to let anyone fix them yet,' I think to myself, smiling at him.

CHAPTER FIVE

Let the rain wash the pain away and bring me hope.

Standing at the bus stop I check my watch, I've been standing here thirty minutes and still no bus! Picking up my shopping bag, I decide to start walking the long journey home just as the heavens open and rain bounces down hard and fast. I drop my shopping bag on the ground, lifting my head up to the rain. Something about the hard water hitting my skin makes me feel alive...

For the first time in a long while I finally feel free, I survived! I'm still breathing, and that's all that matters. I'm cold and wet, and I don't care. My heart races fast, beating hard against my chest.

I hear a hornpipe behind me, spinning around I see it's Billy! Slowly, he pulls up, jumping out his truck. "What are you doing out here?"

"Well, don't laugh, but I was waiting for a bus, which never turned up, so I decided to start walking and, well, as you can see it started raining!" I hold out my arms, spinning around, my lungs filling with heavy, happy breaths.

Billy walks behind me, pulls his jacket around my shoulders, and strokes along my arms as he leans in close to my ear, sending my head into a daze. "A word of advice, check the weather warnings next time. No buses run to the lane in this kind of rain! It floods at the bottom really bad." He picks up my shopping, "and if you don't get home soon, you're going to be swimming there."

I feel like such a fool. He's sitting next to me, laughing, and all I can do is laugh with him. "Flood?" I question.

"Yes, this rain is going to be here for the next two days. The bus won't run to the flood prone areas, and because it stops at the bottom of our lane it won't come. You know, because of the hill? Rain runs down hills..." he looks at me and lets out a huge laugh.

"Okay. Okay, very funny, how am I meant to know that?" I slap his arm as we reach the bottom of our lane.

We both jump out of the truck at the same time and run to my front door. "Quick, my keys are in that bag." I point to the bag Billy is still carrying.

"Shit, Mandy, why put your keys in the bottom?"

"Just shut up, and get the keys!" I quickly hold open the bag while he digs around for them. As soon as he has them we both shoot through the door out of the rain. I stop and turn to him, noting that we're both dripping wet. His grey top sticks to his chest. My heart races with excitement as he moves closer, breathing heavy.

"I should really get out of these wet clothes." I softly say, still looking deep into his eyes.

"Yes, you should definitely get out of them." He moves another step closer to me. My whole body wants to run and hide, but my lips ache to touch his.

I shake myself out of the trance and brush past him. "I'll be right back." Rushing upstairs, I throw my dress on the floor and change into my jeans and t-shirt. Using the time to compose myself, I take a long look in my mirror. *'What am I doing? I can't honestly let anything happen here... can I?'* I grab my oversized hoodie from the closet, and head back down stairs.

"I don't have anything you can change into, except this." I hold up my hoodie, he's still standing at the front door, running his hand through his wet hair.

I grab a towel from the tumble dryer, passing it to him along with the hoodie. "Here, change into this and I'll stick your top in the dryer."

"It's okay, I'll just go back to mine." He pulls his truck keys out of his pocket.

"Don't go yet." I hold onto his arm softly. I don't want him to leave.

Billy moves closer until we're toe-to-toe. His hand cups my chin. "What do you want, Mandy?"

I can't help but look away. "I don't know, Billy." I can feel something between us, I just can't say it out loud.

"You feel it too, don't you?"

I pull away from him slowly, not taking my eyes off his. "I... I don't know what I feel. This is the problem, Billy, I don't know what to feel right now." I walk over to the kitchen counter, turning my back to him, I feel the tears welling up inside me.

"What are you scared of, Mandy? I know you feel this thing growing between us." His hands curl around my waist, turning me around to face him. Tenderly, his lips touch mine just for a moment. Soft.

I panic, pushing him away. Fear roars through my veins at the feeling of his skin touching mine. Old memories flood back, hitting me square in the face. I thought I could forget, but it hits me hard.

"NO! I can't do this, Billy! Please..." I feel everything, every little ping of a heartbeat, every flutter of a butterfly. He makes them all happen.

He pulls away from me slowly, backing off. Now I can feel the tears caressing my cheeks.

"I'm sorry, Mandy, I didn't mean to upset you." And before I have time to speak he is gone.

As much as I want to I don't run after him, instead I drop to my knees, allowing the tears from my past to flow just this once. I beg for freedom, I ache for his touch with ever fiber in my body; I want to be free, to feel again, but my past left permanent scars that won't heal. I thought I could move past this, but I can't.

CHAPTER SIX

Demons come in all shapes and sizes, heroes come with deep blue eyes.

The next morning, I wake still feeling like crap from the night before. My head spun all night after what happened with Billy, and I really don't know how I'm going to deal with it all.

Beast shoots up from the bed, "what is it, boy?" I croak, forcing my eyes open. Sitting up, I can hear the faint sound of a knock on the door.

Jumping up, I run to the window to peer at who would be knocking. Billy stands back from the door on the porch. Holding my finger up indicating I will be a moment, I run to the bathroom to get some clothes on.

"Shit." What do I do? My heart races as I touch my lips, remembering where his pressed mine last night. Smiling, I run downstairs.

"Hello." I pull the door open, peering my head out.

"Sorry to wake you, I just thought we could talk about last night, about what happened? Or I can come back later, if you want?" His voice sounds very sincere.

"Oh, no, it's okay. I just wasn't expecting anyone." I pull the door open for him. "Come in, would you like a cup of tea?" I offer, walking off into the kitchen.

"Can we just sit and talk for a moment, Mandy? I think we need to clear the air." My gaze meets his for a second, something feels different. I watch as he takes a seat on the sofa, rubbing his hands together as if he's nervous.

"What do you want to say, Billy?" I take a seat next to him, everything feels wrong.

"What happened last night shouldn't have, and I'm very sorry."

I fall silent for a moment, embarrassed and a little gutted. "What do you mean, Billy?" I try to act as cool as I can, but inside I'm screaming for him to kiss me again.

"The kiss, it shouldn't have happened, I'm sorry, I took advantage of you that way."

"It's fine. I mean, it's not your fault really, I think we both got a little carried away." I shoot up in my seat, and hurry to the kitchen. "Would you like a drink?" I ask again, biding time to catch my breath. How did I get this thing all wrong?

"Does this mean we are still friends, Mandy?" He slowly walks over to the kitchen.

Friends? Did I get everything wrong last night? I spent most of my evening crying over what happened, and the rest of the night dreaming about him. How can it all be a mistake?

I open the cupboard where I store all my teas. "Yeah, sure, what would you like?" I stretch up, examining the varieties. "I have chamomile, lemon, green tea, strawberry, and peppermint tea." I can feel my cheeks redden as Billy lets out a loud laugh.

"Wow! You have an assortment of tea." He tries

hard to contain his laughter. "Do you have just regular tea or coffee?"

I let the cupboard door handle slip from my grip; slamming it shut. "I don't have coffee, but I have regular tea." I keep my back to him, hiding my embarrassment. He's beginning to aggravate me.

"I'm sorry, I shouldn't have laughed at you, it was very rude. I'm not normally like that. Honest." Turning to face him, I can see the guilt on his face.

Beast comes strolling into the kitchen, following me around with every move I take. Billy can sense he is loyal to me. He watches the dog curiously as it sits by my side while I pour the tea.

"He seems very attached to you."

"I'm starting to feel the same way about him, he has a very lucky owner out there somewhere." I bend down and kiss Beast on the nose.

"So, have you lived here long?" My nose scrunches up with embarrassment. Why did I just ask such a stupid question? What the hell is wrong with me? The guy just flat out rejected me, and I'm sat making small talk with him. Get a grip.

"Pretty much, yeah. I left at sixteen, and came back when I was twenty-three. I've lived in the town all my life though. It's a pretty quiet place to be, and everyone helps each other out, which reminds me, I can come tomorrow and sort that gate for you, if you'd like?" he asks.

"On a Sunday? You're already helping me find Beast's owner. I really shouldn't take up any more of your time, surely your wife or girlfriend will think the worst." I stop myself. *'Why the hell did I just say that?'* He kissed me last night, and shoots me down, so there must be someone else, right?

"No one, I'm completely single. Oh, I just remembered. I need your mobile number to put on the poster."

My face reddens. I'd thrown the device away when Hayley left, she didn't want anything that could compromise my safe place. "I don't have a phone." Embarrassment echoes in my voice.

Billy sits for a moment, and I can see him judging

me. "You don't have a phone?"

"No, I don't have any need for one."

"Okay, what about you, Mandy? Will your husband or boyfriend be joining you in the house soon?" He smiles, trying to make a joke of my earlier comment, but my face changes. A serious nerve has been hit, and I shoot up out of my seat. "I think you need to leave now, Billy, I have things to do" I turn my back to him, moving to the sink, Beast copies.

"I'm sorry, Mandy, it was only a joke." He stands, arms crossed over his chest.

I don't answer him. Playing with the water in the bowl, memories flash before my eyes. Thomas and his venomous tongue spitting insults at me from across the room echoes in my ears. Dropping the plate on the floor, I place my hands over my ears. "GET. OUT!" I scream.

Beast's head shoots up, watching as Billy tries to pick up the broken plate. I fall to the floor, my knees hitting the tiles hard. Beast runs over, sitting himself in-between Billy and me.

"Mandy, what is wrong?" he tries to get closer to me, but Beast stands his ground.

I snap my head and reality hits. I'm brought back when I look in his eyes. Thomas is still punishing me even though I left him. "I. I don't know, I'm so sorry I reacted like that, I don't know what came over me." A tear falls from my cheek, and when I try to stand up Billy reaches out to hold my arm. "Please don't touch me! I'm fine. "

Billy stands still for a moment. "I'll leave," he walks to the door. "Sorry I upset you, Mandy. Again."

I sit watching him turn his back to me, leaving for the second time.

I can't carry on letting Thomas control me. The whole point of leaving is to be free of him, but the reality is, I never will be, not if I let his memories flood my future...

If I'm going to have any kind of life, I need to *survive,* not *suffer*.

CHAPTER SEVEN

One kiss, one touch, one moment.

I spend the next three days locked up at home. I have no contact with Billy nor do I want to; I made a complete fool of myself in front of him. I must have looked like a freak flipping out the way I did. I'm too ashamed to go and apologize to him. He didn't do anything wrong except wanting to get to know me, and deep down I really want to get to know him too. There's something about his touch, so tender and caring, it drowns out all the hurt and pain I carry. In one single moment I felt something I haven't felt in a long time... Wanted.

I pull myself out of bed and go downstairs, Beast following my every move as I wander around the kitchen, preparing breakfast for him. Putting his dish on the floor, I decide to spend my Sunday morning sorting out the back garden— something that always makes me happy. Back home, my garden had been my sanctuary, the place I could always go to stay out of Thomas' way.

After finishing breakfast and getting dressed, I call Beast outside and set out on ridding the garden of all the weeds. The garden itself is huge and goes all the way around the property. The back part has an overgrown lawn area with a rockery at the bottom, and bedding plants all the way up one side. When I reach the bottom of the garden, I notice a small gate. The sound of trickling water triggers my curiosity. Turning to check on Beast, I burst into laughter at the sight of him rolling around in all the cuttings. Turning back to the gate excitement builds up inside me.

It is like a secret garden, a small stream and woodland all around. A personal entrance to a secret escape, as I walk through the woodland I can see that all the cottages have a gate leading to the woods. It is an untouched heaven. I hear the crack of a branch, and when I spin around, I find Beast standing behind me.

"Come on, boy, do you want to explore?"

I follow the never-ending stream as it leads me deeper and deeper into the woodland. The smells of wild flowers surrounding me draws me in. Walking through, I feel more at peace than I ever did before. Beast emerges from the stream, soaking wet, and shakes himself off right next to me, before running off in front.

"Beast! Come on, let's head back." I take in another breath and begin trekking back home. Beast slowly follows behind.

When I reach one of the gates, I hear the mumbling of voices coming from behind it. I take a step closer when his voice echoes through my ear. I'm close enough now to hear and see him.

As I peer through the small gap in the gate, I can see him lounging on a chair at the center of his garden, his hand resting on his chest. As I step closer for a better look at who he's talking to, a branch cracks under my foot, and as I look again I see him hurrying towards the gate, towards me.

'Shit,' I think as I hurry with Beast as fast as I can back to the safety of my own garden. I rest my back against the gate just as I hear the faint sound of his gate opening.

After a few moments of silence, I clear up all the mess I made in the garden and clean Beast up from his adventure in the woods. Standing on the step with my tea, I examine the garden. A figure appears from around the side of the house, making me jump.

"I come in peace." Billy stands tall with his hands up in the air, a guilty smile on his face.

I can't help but smile up at him while taking another sip of my tea. "It's okay, Billy, you're safe."

I watch as he tucks his hands deep into his jeans pockets, his t-shirt clinging tightly to his muscular shoulders. He looks nothing like Thomas. Thomas is short and always very well dressed; he thrives on being clean shaven, with not a hair out of place.

Billy seems to dress casually, and his smile lights up his face. I admire the artwork up his arms; both covered in tattoos. One stands out to me more than the others; a girl's name, 'Malissa', wraps around the top of his arm, surrounded by roses and vines.

"Mandy? Are you okay?" Billy pulls me back from my silent admiring. "You look lost in space."

I shake my head in embarrassment. "Sorry, I get lost in my own thoughts sometimes, joys of being alone I suppose."

Billy follows me into the kitchen. "I only really came to apologize for the other day, Mandy. I shouldn't have made fun of you in the way that I did; I don't think about what I'm doing sometimes." He stops for a moment, brushing his hair back. "I just wanted to make sure you know that I'm very sorry I upset you, and that I hope we can still be friends."

"Billy, you don't have to apologize. Honestly, I overreacted big time. Listen, I just got out of a really messy relationship and I guess I'm still a little on edge about it all. I moved here for a fresh start, and I really appreciate you being the welcoming neighbor."

"I'm glad we're okay now. Before I forget, I'll be here first thing in the morning to start on these jobs you need doing, okay? I hope the other day hasn't changed your mind."

Beast comes running in the house, wagging his tail at Billy. "Hey, boy! Are you my friend again now?" he laughs at Beast's reaction as he rolls over onto his back.

"Of course, I'm looking forward to not having a leaking tap and a gate that slams all through the night." I pour out my tea and stand by the sink.

"Great." He stands up and walks over to the door. "I'll get out of your hair now, I have to get back home. I'll see you at some point tomorrow, Mandy." His hand touches mine as he walks over to the sink, placing his cup in. I feel it instantly; a spark, a feeling, butterflies dancing, and my heart pounding against my chest. It's like my body knows what I want even though I don't. There were times when Thomas touched me that I would cower, my skin would crawl at the feeling, and there were other times my body would shiver, sickness would race up through my gut at the slightest touch. That's what happens when you make someone so scared of you, even a single touch can break them down.

It's not like that when Billy touches me. My biggest fear is how frail and beat down I had become, that a man's touch didn't excite me anymore, it scared me. Yet, somehow, in the few encounters I've had with Billy that fear has washed away with him. I'm not a victim; I'm just me.

CHAPTER EIGHT

You only hurt me when I close my eyes.

I feel the thump of a fist against my cheek, then the pain comes, screaming its way through my body. Thump. Thump. Thump. More pain shoots across my ribs, and then I feel his breath on my neck. I hate that feeling the most.

"Please, Thomas, I'm sorry for what I did."

His lips touch the nape of my neck and his teeth sink in. "You need to learn your lesson, Miranda, and it seems this is the only way I can teach it to you!" His hand forces my head to the floor, pinning me down.

"NO!" I scream, jumping up from the bed. Beast bursts through the door as I take in my surroundings. "Shit, Beast, I'm sorry boy. Did I frighten you?" He sits with his head resting on the edge of the bed. I've had the same nightmare for six days now, and to make things worse, Billy is keeping his distance from me. Looking over at my alarm clock it flickers 07:50.

***

Sitting at the table with my cup in hand, I stare out of the kitchen window. I love the view from here as I can see all the way past my garden, and into the woods behind. I have really grown to love this place, but I miss my home and my friends. It's lonely leaving everything you know behind to start again.

I pull my shrug over my shoulders and snuggle on the sofa with Beast, when I hear a knock on the door. Hoping it's Billy, I rush to open it, and I'm taken by complete surprise. Hayley's standing on my door step.

"Hey, Miranda, got a hug for your friend?" She stands with her arms wide open, waiting for my embrace.

Overtaken by shock, I stand for a moment. I

thought I would never see her again. "Hayley! What are you doing here? I thought we agreed you wouldn't come — it's too dangerous." I pull her in the front door, quickly closing it behind me. "Are you crazy? What if Thomas followed you here?"

"Oh, sweetie, that ship has long sailed. After he told the whole neighborhood he caught you with another man and threw you out, he went on to move his little tart into the house, and according to her they have been sleeping together for the past three years. And besides, everyone thinks I'm off at the spa for the day." Dropping her bag in the hall, she strolls off into the kitchen, and places the kettle on the stove. "He came knocking at my door the morning you left, but Adam told him I was asleep in bed, and that I had been all night. He asked me if I had heard from you, but I just told him if I did hear from you I wasn't going to tell him anyway."

"He moved her in? That man has no shame." I slump down at the table next to her, holding my head in my hands. "You know, I checked the bank accounts, and he's locked me out of them all, except for mine that is."

"Can he fight you for the money? You know, if you manage to get him to divorce you?"

I feel a big smile spreading across my face. "He can't touch a penny of what my mother left for me, and he wouldn't dare fight me for it because the house, and everything in it, all belong to me. I even invested in his business right at the start, so if he ever thought about fighting me I could take everything away from him, and his little money-grabbing bit on the side." I settle back in the chair, feeling completely happy with myself at the security blanket I surrounded myself with upon getting married to him.

"Wait, you knew about her? And you never said!" Hayley places her hand on mine, her touch finned with symbol. "When did you find out?"

"About two years ago. One night I was too tired and refused to sleep with him, so he turned to me and told me he would go and see his girlfriend—she knew just how he liked it." I remember that night most of all. He beat me black and blue for not sleeping with him, then spat on me before leaving to go and have sex with another woman. After that night he kept out of my way in the bedroom department, unless he was drunk and desperate.

Hayley potters around the kitchen, mumbling under her breath about what a bastard he is while she makes a cup of tea. Beast comes running in from out back, making her jump. "What the hell is that, Miranda!?"

"This is Beast, my bodyguard." I laugh out loud, patting my leg for him to come and sit with me. "He isn't much of a bodyguard though, not when you've been in the house ten minutes before he realized."

"Well, he definitely suits his name. He looks bloody scary." She follows me out to the garden to my new bench. "It's so quiet out here," she says.

"I love it. It's peaceful, and relaxing, and a major

shame it's not going to be permanent." I know I will be leaving as soon as I sort my divorce, but deep down a part of me doesn't want to leave. The thought of leaving Beast and Billy leaves a sense of sadness in me. I keep telling myself this is just temporary, but I'm not very convincing.

"What is it, Miranda? What's going on in that head?" Hayley knows me all too well. She can see me slipping from reality and into my own little world.

"I don't know, Hayley. It's just everything." I take a sip of my tea.

"You don't still have feelings for him, do you?"

"Of course not! How could you ask me that?" Anger fills up inside me, I stand, taking in a deep breath. "I feel nothing for that monster, he's not the man I fell in love with and married. I fell in love with my school sweetheart; a kind, gentle man that cherished me, and worshiped the ground I walked on. And now look at me, I'm living with a vine of thorns wrapped around my heart because I fear being hurt again. I'm I have nothing left, Hayley. I'm so scared of him finding me, or of someone else even touching me again... And then there's Billy..." I'm about to begin explaining about Billy when I hear a rustling from the side of the house. When he comes out into the garden my heart stops instantly, butterflies dancing about inside, and my hands begin to twitch, itching for just one touch. What the hell is happening to me? I freeze, watching his pearly green eyes as he comes around and introduces himself to Hayley. All the while his eyes are fixed on me, staring at me with that stern look about him.

"So, I take it you're Billy? My dear friend Miranda was just about to tell me all about you." She turns to inspect my reaction.

Billy folds his arms across his chest and looks at me with a frowned look upon his face. I try to move closer to him, but he moves away. *Why the hell did* an empty shell, surviving each day as it comes.

she just call me Miranda?

"Well, *Miranda*," I sense the sarcasm in his tone. "I'll leave and your friend to it..." He turns to walk away.

"Billy, wait!" I chase him through the house and grab hold of his arm, pulling him back. "Wait... let me explain."

"Explain what, Miranda?"

"What the hell is your problem with me?" My breath feels heavy as I hold on tight for an answer.

"Listen, Mandy, Miranda, whatever your name is, I don't know who you are but please don't use me in this game you're playing with your husband. I came over to tell you how I really feel about you, and then I overhear you talking about being in love with this mysterious guy that worships the ground you walk on...don't use me as a pawn in your stupid marital game.

He pulls my hand from his arm and storms out the door.

I try to chase after him, but my feet won't move. "Billy, wait! I need you to listen to me," I shout to him, but it falls on deaf ears. He's already gone.

CHAPTER NINE

Can a shattered heart be fixed?

Hours have passed. Hayley has long since gone home, and I sit curled up on the sofa feeling empty and confused. If only I had been honest with him from the start, none of this would've happened. As I look over to the clock I let out a sigh. "Seven o'clock, Beast. What do you say we go for a quick walk? Maybe the fresh air will clear my head a little?" He tilts his head as I reach for his lead and open the front door.

Walking past Billy's house, I can see the light on. My feet move to the door before my head has time to think, and I'm knocking on the door. Pulling my shrug around me tight, I wait for him to answer. When the door opens, the sight takes my breath away. His smile lights up the night sky, and then his eyes fall on me. The smile disappears and once again he frowns at the sight of me. My heart drops into my stomach.

"Billy, please, I need to explain something to you, then I'll leave, and I won't bother you again. Please just listen first."

"Fine! You have ten minutes." He moves aside, indicating for me to step inside. He leads me into the sitting room and closes the door behind us.

Okay, here is my chance. A chance to open up and trust someone enough to tell them exactly what my life has been like for the last ten years. My hands begin to shake, I sit up, and take a deep breath. It's time to admit the truth to myself.

"My real name is Miranda Chase. I'm twenty-eight years old, and yes, I did love my husband, but not anymore, he's not that man anymore. The truth is..." I pause for a second, and time stands still. "The truth is I've been abused by my husband for the last ten years, and when my friend Hayley found out she helped me get me away. She's the *only* person that has any idea what I've gone through. She's the only person I could ever talk to about it. I was a very naïve girl when we began our relationship, and when we married he wanted me to honor and obey everything he said. I wasn't allowed to answer back, I was made to do as I was told, always, and I was there to please him as and when he needed." A single tear trickles down my cheek at the admission.

"I finally left because if I hadn't he probably would've killed me, or I would've killed myself! And I mean that very seriously, Billy. The reason I flipped out the other day when you tried to touch me is because the thought of anyone touching me freaks me out, my abuse hasn't always been physical. In fact, just the opposite. He hates to leave any kind of mark on his perfect little wife, but what he does enjoy doing is grinding me down 'til there's nothing left. I'm weak! I'm stupid! I'm ugly! I'm useless…. The worst of my abuse came when I fell pregnant, not because he abused me, but because I only had one choice. I had to break my own heart have an abortion. I could never bring a child into that kind of world."

I stand up, rubbing my clammy hands together. The memories flood back all at once, and I feel my heart ripping into tiny pieces. Billy stands up, slowly walking over towards to me. My feet give way on me, but his arms reach out and catch me before I fall. "I'm okay, Billy." I pull myself back up as he guides me to the sofa. "I told you I would tell you the truth and that's it. You are different from anyone else I've ever met, and I didn't want you to look at me like a victim...just like you're looking at me now."

The room falls into silence. I want to say so much more, but the words are muddled up in my mind. Billy sits beside me and places his hand on mine; the reassurance in his touch feels real.

"I never told him about what I did, and the abuse carried on regardless. I soon found out that he has a secret girlfriend, a second life. I hoped that he'd leave me or at least stop the abuse. It didn't." I have to stop. The thoughts of what I put myself through, the pain of living with a man you know didn't love you is too much. I can't help the tears that cascade down my cheeks.

Billy's hand caresses my cheek. "Mandy. You really don't need to explain any more. I'm sorry I jumped to conclusions about your life, I had no right."

My mind races as his touch erases everything I want to say. I reach up until my lips touch his, and I fall into a sense of euphoria as my lips move in rhythm with his. Both my hands reach up, running through his hair. Before I have time to think, his hands are moving around my waist, pulling me into his lap. I freeze as his hands stroke down my back.

I jump from his lap. "I'm so sorry, Billy...I just can't... I'm sorry..." I hurry my words out, wrapping the shrug back over my shoulders and rush towards the door.

"Mandy, wait! What's wrong?"

He runs in front of me, pressing himself against the door, blocking my exit.

I dip my head in shame. "Billy, I came here tonight to tell you the truth. Not for you to take pity on me, and not to seduce you with my sob story..."

"Mandy, I didn't kiss you because I felt sorry for you, and I don't think you did the seducing either! I kissed you because I wanted to, just like I have wanted since that night you turned up on my door with Beast... You have this hold over me that I just can't explain, but it's like when I see you I want you.... *all* of you." He takes a step closer, his hands stroking the sides of my arms. "If you're not ready then I respect your choice, but I will be waiting, I'll be waiting right here until you decide you're ready to let me love you."

His lips gently touch the side of my cheek, he steps aside from the door.

The only thing I can do is walk away, not looking back at him once.

When I reach my house, I'm walking like a zombie up the stairs to my room. I have so many emotions running through my head I can't think straight. I hate myself for leaving like that, even after what he said. I'm a coward for running away.

I flop backwards on the bed, drifting off to sleep with Beast curled up beside me.

Chapter Ten

Breaking the chains around my heart.

I've kept myself hauled up in my house for the past two days, my heart aching, head hurting, and my body exhausted. Each day I stand by the spare bedroom window, watching Billy walk through the woods out back, scurrying away out of sight each time he looks up at my house.

I can't escape the conflicted emotions running through my mind. I haven't had feelings like this in a long time. No, scrap that, I've *never* had feelings like this, never had someone give me such butterflies when I see them, no one has ever made me want them this much before. It hurts.

I'm tired of the fear, tired of convincing myself he will only hurt me just like Thomas. I'm tired of convincing myself he only wants me because he feels sorry for me. I want to feel the love he proclaims to feel, I want to feel wanted, to feel his soft touch, his lips on mine. I want to feel the freedom he offers. Is it so wrong to feel so alive in someone else's arms?

The question hangs in my mind as I creep along the cold, wood flooring to the spare room once again, standing at the window in nothing but bare feet and a nightgown. I pull the curtain back inch by careful inch, watching, waiting.

My heart races as a few minutes later he appears, walking with his hands deep inside his jeans pockets, slowly strolling through the overgrown grass, dandelions blowing in the morning breeze as he passes by them. I hitch a breath at the sight of him, the sky fully open to the sunshine without a cloud to shadow him. This time I can't pull away from the window when he stops to look up at my house. I just stand staring at him, no fears, no worries, just a feeling of want and need rush through my veins. He slowly brushes his fingers through his tussled hair as he stands, staring up at me with the same need in his eyes as my own.

This time, I'm the one forcing my feet to move, rushing down the stairs as fast as I can, I fumble with the lock at the back door.

I dash down the garden path, flinging the gate open, slamming it shut behind me. Holding on to the bottom of my nightgown, I run as fast as I can through the dandelions, jumping up into his open arms, and wrap my legs around his waist as tight as I can.

Our lips silently declare what we both feel for each other as we kiss. This time, I don't freak out, I don't run and hide. I embrace his touch, bathing in the tenderness.

I lower myself from his hold and stand on my own two feet in front of him, hating the breeze that blows between us.

"Billy, I'm sorry I pushed you away." His finger gently presses on my lips, stopping me in the middle of my sentence.

"None of that matters now. I told you I would wait — I wanted to tell you so much more, but I couldn't find the words. I wanted you to be sure this is what you want, I didn't want you to think I just said it because I felt sorry for what happened to you."

Taking hold of my hand, he walks me back through my garden, and into the house.

Both his hands reach up, resting on both my cheeks. "The reason I came over the other day was to tell you I had fallen for you, and I completely blew it."

"So, say it now," I whisper under his touch.

"You are beautiful." His lips touch my neck, kissing softly.

"You are smart." Next, they touch behind my ear.

"You are caring." His eyes drift off to look in Beasts direction.

"You make my whole-body sing when you look

at me with those gorgeous, hazel eyes." His lips meet mine ever so softly, touching before pulling away again.

His gaze deepens, staring into my soul. "And you are the strongest woman I have ever met."

When his lips touch mine they don't stop, his kiss is full of passion, so much so my whole body aches for him, for more.

For a moment he stops, pulling his lips away from mine. "Are you sure you want this, Mandy?" His tongue trails down my neck, completely distracting me from what I want to say, his fingers trace the straps on my nightdress, pushing them down. I shrug and let it drop down my body slowly.

"Billy, I don't want to think. Just make me feel again. Please!" I bury myself deeper into his kiss until I fall completely.

Before I have time to think he pulls me to my feet, cupping my breast in his hand. His tongue dances across my nipple, my knees buckle under his touch. He pulls me into his arms, carrying me all the way to the top of the stairs.

"Billy, please..." I beg him, tugging at his t-shirt.

With one look, he pushes the door open and leads me towards the bed. His eyes never fade from mine as he strips me of everything, including all the guards I put up.

His lips taste every inch of my body, washing away all the damage Thomas had done. My body becomes alive.

CHAPTER ELEVEN

You can't hurt me anymore.

I lay wrapped in Billy's arms for the longest time, listening to the sound of his heart beating, strong and steady like the rhythm of a drum. God, this man makes me feel something I have never felt before. He's emptied my beaten heart of the hurt and filled it with something I haven't felt in years. I try to move free from his grasp, but he pulls me closer, his eyes firmly shut. I know he isn't asleep; I can see his eyelids flutter as he tries to keep the smile off his face.

Days have passed since we silently declared our true feeling for each other, neither of us wanting to admit it out loud, but both knowing how the other really feels. Magic passes between us each time we are together, and every single worry I had washed away that morning.

The nights I spent reliving my horrors are now a thing of the past— I no longer wake, feeling the pain all over again. Not when I'm wrapped in Billy's arms, I no longer fear his touch. I welcome and embrace it.

"Billy, I really should go home." I sit up, pulling the sheet around me. I take in his beauty one last time, and then pry myself from his grasp.

He stretches out, catching my arm, his grip firm but longing. "Do you really have to go home now? Why don't you just stay here tonight and then go home in the morning?"

When I turn to look at him, an outburst of laughter escapes my lungs. His lip curls down, pouting like a baby, begging me to stay.

"I really need to take Beast home and get some sleep. I wriggle free from his grip once again, searching around the room for my clothes.

Billy stands up behind me, his arms firm around my waist. What I wouldn't give to stay here the night with him. "Billy, I love waking up to your smile in the morning, but I really do need to go home and get some sleep. So much has happened, I think we both need to think about where we go from here."

He pauses for a moment, then pulls me back over to the bed.

"Can I just lay here in your arms for the rest of my life?" I shuffle down the bed, resting my head back on his chest while his hand strokes up and down my back.

"You can lay here as long as you like, you are in complete control of where this all goes, Mandy."

"I like the sound of that." I smile and drift into a deep, dreamless sleep.

***

I'm woken from my slumber with the feeling of soft lips touching my cheek. Opening my eyes, I breathe in the scent of him hovering over me.

"Morning."

"Morning to you, too." He flops down on the

bed beside me. "What plans do you have today?"

I turn over to face him, resting my head on my hand. "Nothing at all. Why?"

"Fancy picnic? There's something kind of important I need to tell you..." he trails off and climbs out of bed.

"Sure, sounds good," I respond nervously. "I'll Just jump in the shower."

After a hot shower I throw on my leggings and top, pulling my dolly shoes on. Something pulls at my gut. What is so important that he needs to tell me about? My mind races. I rush downstairs, watching as he dashes around the kitchen, packing us lunch into a basket.

I clear my throat to gain his attention.

He spins around, his gaze meeting mine. "Hey, you look beautiful."

"Thank you." I walk over to him and rest my lips on his.

"Come on, let's go." He breaks away from the kiss, grabbing my hand he pulls me through the back door and down to the bottom of his garden. I know exactly where we're going.

We make the short journey through the woodland to the open field with the stream running calmly. Billy takes the blanket out from the top of the basket, and lays it on the floor. Unpacking all the food, I can see his hand shaking.

Placing my hands on his, I stop him, pulling him down to sit on the blanket for a moment. "Billy, whatever it is you need to tell me, just tell me." I reassure him.

"I wanted to tell you so many times before now, but I always chickened out." He released his hands from mine, running them through his hair, something I've noticed he does when he's nervous.

"Billy, just tell me..." My hand presses on the side of his cheek for a moment, and I smile at him.

"I have a daughter..."

I take in his confession for a moment, replaying his sentence in my mind. Malissa...that explains the tattoo. "Okay."

"She's five years old and lives with her mother." He dips his head down in shame.

I place my hand on his chin, turning him to look at me, I can see the pain in his eyes. "Start from the beginning..." I ask.

"Remember when I told you I left, and came back when my granddad died?"

I simply nod, still holding his cheek.

"Well, when I was away, I married my childhood girlfriend. She got a place at Manchester university, so we decided we could move there together. Everything was going well, she finished university and got a really great job, I started my own gardening business, and then Malissa was born... We began to drift apart. When my grandad became ill, I was needed back here more and more. Eventually, I was spending weeks here, leaving her to deal with Malissa, the house and work. I begged her to come with me, but she couldn't." He pauses for a moment, taking a breath.

"One weekend I brought Malissa with me to give

her a break, but when we returned I caught her in bed with another guy. She'd been sleeping with him for months while I was gone. After that we tried to make it work but it didn't. We screamed and shouted at each other, constantly blaming one another for our mistakes. When my grandad died, I decided I was needed more here than I was there, so I left."

Anger filled up inside me, hurt by his pain. "You mean she cheated on you and you lost out on your daughter, business and home? How is that fair, Billy?"

He stood up and began pacing back and forth through the long grass. "It wasn't like that, Mandy! I let her down. What husband leaves his wife and baby week after week? What husband lets his business fail? I couldn't be there for her when she needed me, I don't blame her for seeking another man for what I couldn't give her. I blame myself for failing them both!" He stops for a moment and sits back down on the blanket with me.

"I moved back here, and believe me, it really works for us. Malissa comes here to stay with me in the holidays, and I go there to visit her at the weekends when I'm not busy. We are better parents apart than we ever were together."

"Billy, how could you ever think that you failed? It takes two people to make a marriage work or crumble. She failed you just as much."

Billy sat for a moment and began unpacking the food again. "Is that how you feel about your own marriage? That you both failed?"

His question leaves me stunned. "In a way, yes. I think I failed the day I said 'I do'! Thomas changed the day we married. Did I deserve what I got? No! But could I have stopped it happening? In all honesty, I could've got out a lot sooner than I did." My own confession pains me. Deep down I admit I could have left a long time before I did, but when someone has that hold over you, all the strength in the world wouldn't have been enough to set me free.

We both sit in silence at our past lives, both pained with memories of failure and heartache. Deep down we are both recovering.

I lay back on the blanket, resting my hand on my stomach.

Laying down next to me, Billy places his hand over mine. "Does this change what we have?"

"Yes and no."

"How so?"

"I still love you, Billy, my feelings won't change just because you have a past. Look at me, yet you still want to be with me knowing the damage that's been done. It both excites me and scares me that you have a daughter. Deep down the only question running through my head is where does this leave us as a couple? I know we haven't spoken about the future, and we're just taking each day slowly. but it's a big change having that kind of commitment in the middle of us."

"It changes nothing, Mandy, the reason I told you is because I want you to be a part of this, I want you to be part of my future and of my past. Malissa is always going to be my number one priority, I couldn't ever put anyone before her. That's why I had to make sure my feelings for you were real and that you felt the same way about me. I would never let women come and go in my daughter's life."

Laying side by side, we both breathe a heavy sigh of relief.

Chapter Twelve

More pain than one can bare.

My house feels empty and cold without him here. Throwing my keys on the table, I decide to jump in the shower before Billy brings Beast back from his walk. A cold breeze blows in from the kitchen, rushing to the back door I notice I must have left it open. Shrugging, I shut it and turn off the lights, making my way to the stairs.

When I reach the bathroom, I turn on the shower and go to my bedroom, getting fresh clothes ready. Something deep inside me didn't feel right, I didn't feel alone.

Bang!

The sound of my door slamming makes me jump, I spin around and come face to face with a monster. I can't run, I'm frozen.

"Hello, dear wife!" That voice, it makes the hairs on my neck stand up. "Haven't we been up to no good?"

Fear shoots through me, gripping at my chest. "How did you find me, Thomas? What do you want?" Panic strikes me as I try to run for the door. His arms fling around me, pulling me into his tight hold.

"Why should you have all the fun, Miranda? I've been watching you prancing around with that new boyfriend of yours. Quite the looker, isn't he?" His words hiss out as he grips my chin, forcing me to look him in the eyes. I try to fight free of him, but his hold is too tight.

His tongue strokes up my cheek, making me squirm even more. "I don't want to go home with you! Just leave me alone." Pushing my arms out, I release myself from his hold, trying to run for the door. He pulls me back, throwing me to the other side of the room. Pain rumbles through my head as it slams against the wall, my feet buckle and I drop to the floor.

Cowering in the corner of the room, I tuck my knees close to my chest, praying for Billy to come quickly.

"You belong to me, Miranda! And you will be coming home with me one way or another." He steps closer, bending down in front of me he tilts his head to the side and smiles. "God, you look pathetic!"

"STOP IT!" I cover my ears with my hands as he laughs at me. "Just leave me alone."

His hands grip onto mine, pulling them away from my ears as he drags me to the centre of my room. "You are my wife, and you will start acting like my fucking wife! Do you understand? You will never be rid of me. You really thought you could cut me out of everything and then just run away?" I feel his weight resting on my stomach as he leans in closer.

"Thomas, stop! You're hurting me." I scream out. Trying to wriggle out of his grip.

"I'm not leaving until you learn you belong to me! And only me. No one will ever love you."

Laying on my back on the cold, wood floor, I feel like I'm stuck in another nightmare. The anger on his face sends fresh fear through me.

His hand stings the side of my cheek, leaving a burning mark.

His tongue trails down my cheek.

He reaches for my arms, pinning them above my head while his other hand makes its way along the side of my body. "Aren't we the little tart? Wonder if you will give it to me as easily as you gave it to him!" His fingers slide up my dress, stroking the top my knickers.

"Get off me! HELP!" I yell out. "Get the fuck off me, Thomas!"

"Shut up, you little fucking tart, and don't move a muscle!" He lifts my head and then slams it down on the floor. Everything goes blurry. "You really think you could walk out on me and I wouldn't find you? I followed that little bitch from next door here, I knew she would lead me to you."

The pain in my chest is all too much as a screeching pain hits me across the face. I can't move. I try to scream for help, but I can't breathe anymore. My body is in so much pain, I can't even struggle anymore. The sound of his zipper opening curdles my blood.

I can hear faint scratching from the other side of the bedroom door, and hope builds up inside me.

"BEAST!" I scream from deep inside.

Finally, Beast bursts his way through the door, running right towards us, and bites down hard on Thomas' arm, dragging him off me. I scurry to my feet, holding on tight to my stomach, I rush to the bedroom door, but the pain is too much, my knees buckle, and I drop to the floor just at the top of the stairs.

"Mandy!" I hear Billy faintly shouting from the front door.

"Billy." I shout as loud as I can, but my throat hurts.

He reaches me at the top of the stairs, bending down I see a darkness in his eyes, and he darts a look towards the bedroom and back to me. Wrapping my arm around his shoulder, he pulls me to my unsteady feet, and moves towards the screams coming from the bedroom. I hold myself up against the doorframe, and Thomas tries to shake Beast off his arm.

"Get this fucking mutt off my arm!" He snarls towards Billy.

"Beast! It's okay, boy, I'll deal with him." Billy pulls the dog off Thomas and punches him, I jump at the sound of his fist connecting with skin and bones. Closing my eyes tightly, Beast rushes over to my side.

Thomas is stronger, and with Beast out of the way, he swings at Billy, pushing him into the wall.

"Mandy, get out of here!" Billy shouts as he tries to hold Thomas in his grip. I limp to the top of the stairs with help from Beast, but Thomas is rushing over, grabbing my hair, he tries to pull me back.

"Get the hell off her right now, you piece of shit!" Billy runs, pulling Thomas out of my reach, Beast stands in front of me, snarling with all his fur stood up on his back.

"It's okay, Mandy, the police are on their way." Billy declares, just as Thomas loosens from his grip and lunges towards me once again. This time Billy is ready for him, and pulls his arm, twisting it around his back, forcing him to the other end of the room.

He punches Thomas repeatedly until he eventually falls to the floor. Beast stands in front of him, barking, growling, doing everything to keep him from moving. Thomas lays on the floor defeated.

"My God, Mandy, what has he done to you?" Billy scoops me into his arms and carries me over to the bed, gently laying me down. His tender fingers brush my tangled, blood-soaked hair out of my face.

I try to smile through the pain, but the taste of

blood in my mouth is making me feel sick. "Billy," I try to speak but his fingers brush over my lip, stopping me.

The last thing I hear before blacking out is the sirens chasing down the lane.

CHAPTER THIRTEEN

Should I stay, or should I go?

Faint light wakes me; I feel his fingers wrap around mine. "Billy?" I ask, slowly opening my eyes. My throat feels dry as I try to pull myself up the bed. "Where am I?"

Billy slides onto the bed, curling himself up next to me. "It's okay, Mandy, you're in the hospital. That fucker did a real number on you." I feel his lips press down on my forehead. "Just let me go and get the doctor."

I try to keep a hold of his hand, but he pulls away from me and leaves out the door. I sit up in the bed, instantly regretting it as the pain in my ribs tear through my body. Memories from the bedroom battle come flooding in. If Beast hadn't been there with me, God knows what Thomas would have done. He could have killed me.

I try to stretch over and get the glass of water off the side table just as Billy comes in the room, and scoots around the bed, grabbing the water for me and holding it to my lips.

"The doctor is coming to see you in a minute." He places the cup back on the table, and sits on the bed, once again stroking my hair. "God, Mandy, I was so scared when I heard you screaming. I wanted to kill him when I saw what he'd done to you."

"How did you know I was in trouble, Billy?"

"I just got back to mine from walking Beast, and he started acting really strange, like he knew something was wrong with you. He was frantic, jumping up and down, pulling at my leg. I walked him down the lane, and he charged off through your front door and that's when I heard you screaming. I rang nine-nine-nine, and ran in." He took hold of my hand, kissing it softly. "When I reached the top steps and saw you curled up on the floor like that..." he shakes his head, "and once

I realized Beast had a hold of that fucker, I flipped out and went for him."

I knew Beast was special but if he wasn't around, I could've been dead. No one would've known what was happening to me.

***

I have a visit from the doctor, telling me I can go home in a couple of days. They inform me I've suffered two broken ribs, a concussion and several cuts and bruises to my face, legs and arms. After they gave me an x-ray showing old breaks, the doctor told me they would have to repost the previously visible injuries to the police.

A few hours later a police officer came and informed me that Thomas will be formally charged. To my shock, not just for actual bodily harm, but attempted rape as well. He told me I can use the previous abuse as evidence against him too if I want, which will help me gain a restraining order when he eventually gets out of prison. Yes, prison.

Thomas is finally, after ten years, getting what he deserves.

As we arrive back at the house, Billy jumps out of his seat and runs around the truck to help me out. As soon as my feet touch the floor, Beast comes running towards me. "Hey, boy." I painfully lean forward to stroke his ears. "Who's a little hero?"

"He definitely is." Billy walks me into the house.

I stop dead in my tracks, grabbing hold of his arm. "Can we just go to yours? Please? I don't want to go back in there just yet. I'm not ready."

"Come on, I'll make you a chamomile tea. That *is* the relaxing one, isn't it?" he nudges my arm, giving me that smile I could melt into.

I sit down on the sofa, curling myself up into a ball. I can't hold back my tears any longer as all bad pours out.

Billy rushes over. taking me in his arms. "Don't cry, baby."

'*Baby.*' No one has called me baby in a long

time, not since my dad stopped talking to me. Billy presses his lips on my forehead, and I instantly melt into his touch. I can't help myself as I curl my fingers through his hair, and pull his lips to meet mine. A kiss sent from heaven, and I had fallen fast.

Billy pulls away, taking hold of either side of my face. "Mandy, I love you."

His lips lock on mine with so much force, I swear the earth stands still until it ends. When he stops kissing me, I bury my head under his arms, and let my eyes stare around the room. A dark shadow looms over my house now as that too has been filled with bad memories of a broken, beaten heart. No matter where I go Thomas continues to taint my path with his venom.

I had a life before this place. A family, friends, but now I have a new life, one with a man that I'm in love with. Do I stay and build a life here in the place I love, with a man that saved my life? Or do I go back and rebuild from the beginning?

I know one thing for sure. I want Billy in my life. I

fell fast for him, and I don't want to give Mandy up.

She's stronger than Miranda, she survived.

CHAPTER FOURTEEN

Take it slow or lose it.

As I sit curled up, my mind begins to drift to all that has happened over the past few weeks. Life with Billy seems too easy, almost like I'm going to wake up any moment, and all this is going to disappear.

"Hey, sleepy head." Billy leans over me. "Can we talk?"

I slowly sit up. "What is it, Billy?"

He saunters over to the fire and places more logs on it. "We need to talk about what happened."

I stand up, wrapping the shawl around me for both comfort and warmth. I can feel the tears rolling down my cheeks, is this it? The dream is over and I'm going to wake in the nightmare once again.

"What's the matter, Mandy?" Billy's hand curls around my waist, holding me tight. "Hey, look at me. What's wrong?" He turns me round to look at him, reaching up, I wrap my arms around his neck, pulling him closer I rest my head on his shoulder and let my tears run, not saying a word.

"Mandy, talk to me." He lifts my chin to look at him. "Is it too soon?"

Shaking my head in protest, I take a deep breath. "It's everything."

"What do you mean, everything?" He questions, our bodies begin rocking side to side, like dancing to an invisible beat.

"I mean all of this, is it all real? I've been lost for so long, I can't seem to grasp that all this is real?"

Billy stops for a moment, brushing the hair off my face, he tucks it behind my ear. "Mandy, this right here, right now, is real. Me and you are real! You need to stop doubting yourself and us. I don't know what future we have together, but I have told you before, you are in charge of whatever happens. You want it to end tomorrow? I won't stop you. You want to spend the rest of your life curled up in my arms? I'll be there." His palm rests on my cheek. "I love you, Mandy, and nothing will change that, but you need to stop letting your past keep you from having a future."

"I know I do, Billy, but I don't know how to."

"You think I don't hear you and those nightmares you keep having? You're so scared of everything you have, you cry most of the night about it. You think I don't know what's running through your mind right now? You think I don't see the worry in your eyes when you wake every morning? I know what you're thinking now, and that's why I'm holding you. Mandy, last night is the first night I have spent away from you since Thomas, and I don't think I can ever spend a single night away from you ever again, but for us to move forward you need to let go...you need to talk to me, stop bottling it all up, and just let me be the one to take all the pain and fear away from you."

"This is everything I ever wanted, Billy. This is what I should have had. Why did I deserve to live in

Hell for ten long years? I didn't do anything wrong, so why did I have to live that way for so many years? I don't know how to be happy! I just know how to pretend to be."

I stand up, and walk to the kitchen, taking a bottle of wine out the fridge. I walk back with two glasses.

He walks up behind me, turning me to face him. "Mandy, you don't have to pretend anymore. I'm here, with you, for as long as you want me. I will never hurt you, please believe me." He cups my face, his finger traces along my lip so gently I feel my whole body melt to his touch.

As we spend the next few hours curled up close together, he rests his head on my lap, telling me all about his amazing little girl, about all the wonderful things they have done together, and how she will be coming to visit him in a week. A part of me loves the idea of having her here, but then a part of me wants to run to the corner and hide. The shameful part of me is jealous at what Billy has, something I so desperately want but will never have. This part scares me, because this is the part of me that could end me and Billy.

Beast sits on the floor in front of the fire, and I can feel Billy drifting off to sleep. I run my fingers through his hair, taking in this quiet, peaceful moment. I'm utterly thankful for what I have around me. I've come a long way in the few months I have been here. My choice to stay didn't come easy, I miss my friends and my family greatly, but I need this clean start with Billy.

CHAPTER FIFTEEN

Tiny fingers, big heart.

My palms are sweaty, and I'm nervous as hell. I stand in front of the mirror for the tenth time, arranging my hair and dress. Running down stairs, I check the cupcakes in the oven. Beast is sat right beside the oven, waiting for his share of them.

"Come on, Beast, you know you can't have any of these, they will make you into a big, lazy dog."

I look over and check the clock once more, 10:30. *'Crap, they'll be here any minute!'* I straighten my dress one last time, and make my way to the door, waiting for my guest to arrive.

Billy stopped at his place last night so that he could set off early to go and pick Malissa up. I've missed him so much, it's the longest we've been away from each other since.

I can hear Billy's truck coming down the lane. I

take a deep breath as he pulls up outside my house, waving his hand at me. He walks around to the passenger side, throwing me a wink as he opens the door.

Taking hold of her tiny hand, he walks by her side up my garden path, throwing me a smile, they stop in front of me. "Malissa. this is Mandy, the lady I told you about."

I slowly bend down in front of her. "Hey, Malissa, it's lovely to finally meet you, your dad has told me so much about you."

I hold my hand out in front of her.

"Hello, Mandy." Her little hand shakes mine.

I stand and look at Billy.

"Shall we head inside, baby girl?"

I step aside and let them both head in before me, as soon as she sets eyes on Beast sitting by the fire, she rushes over and instantly sits beside him, stroking him over and over.

"He loves that!" I tell her.

Billy stands, leaning on the wall outside the

kitchen, his arms crossed over his chest. I stand watching him for a moment, a tingle of butterflies flutter around inside.

"We'll just be in the kitchen Malissa." He looks back over to me, grabs my hand and pulls me around the corner into the kitchen out of her view. His lips lock onto mine.

"I've missed you, Mandy! I couldn't wait to kiss you again." He lifts me up, pulling me closer to him.

"I've missed you too, Billy, although Beast doesn't snore as much as you!" I chuckle as I try to release his grip.

"You cheeky..." he stops himself, grabbing my hand he pulls me in for another kiss.

Seconds later Malissa creeps in the kitchen. "What's up, baby girl?" Billy bends down in front of her.

"I'm hungry, daddy," she shrugs her shoulders while playing with the bottom of her dress.

"Well, it's a good job I baked all these cakes." I pull the cooled cupcakes off the counter top and place them on the table. "The only problem is I think they need some icing, don't you?" I pull out the chair and wait for her to sit next to me. "Would you like to help?"

Her head nods up and down quickly. "Yes, please."

I sit with Malissa, decorating the cupcakes while Billy makes her a sandwich. I can see him smiling over at us as she tells me all about her cake making skills, and all the names of her friends from school. I stop for a moment and watch as she delicately pipes a bone shape onto one of the cupcakes out of pink icing.

"Is that for Beast?" I smile at her.

She nods at me, trying not to lose her concentration.

"Would you like to take him for a walk with me after lunch?"

"Yes, please!" she shoots her head up.

I can't help but smile over my shoulder at Billy as a single tear builds up in the corner of my eye, this is perfect. This is how it should have been from the start. This is the life I deserved, not the one I had been given.

"Are you okay, Mandy?" Her tiny hand rests on mine for a moment. "Why are you crying?"

Billy places his hands on my shoulders, the gesture of security in his touch only forces more tears.

"They are happy tears, Malissa, that's all. I'm just really happy to finally meet you." I give her a small smile, and turn my attention back to the cakes. "Okay, I think we are done here, I'm just going to wash the dishes and then we can take Beast for a walk. Why don't you go sit in the living room with him, and you can give him his cake if you like."

Smiling, she grabs the cake and hurries into the living room with Beast rushing after her.

Picking up the plates, I walk over to the sink, resting my hands on either side to steady myself.

I stand, listening to Malissa in the other room

talking to Beast as though he could really understand what she was saying, and let out a laugh.

"This is everything I ever wanted, Billy. This is what I should have had...

Wrapping his hands around my waist, Billy caresses my neck with his lips. "You can't think about the journey you took to get to us, you have to think about the journey we are going to take together." His lips, still kissing the nape of my neck, make my head spin.

Turning around, I throw my arms over his shoulders, giggling as we listen to Malissa telling Beast that she's sleeping in my spare room tonight and he can sleep with her.

"I think someone else is in love, too." He whispers in my ear, sending a shiver of excitement from the tips of my toes through my entire body.

"Yeah, and who else is in love?" I question him.

"I think we both know you're madly in love with

me!"

"Yeah, maybe just a little bit!" I pull myself from his hold, and run into the garden. He follows behind me, grabbing hold of my arm and spins me to face him.

"Just a little bit?" His lips once again trail the nape of my neck, and across my collar bone, desire answers his question for him. "Just as I thought. Your lips might say a little, but I can feel your heart beating hard against your chest. Your body's crumbling under my touch."

Taking hold of my hand, he places it firmly on his chest. "Don't worry, baby, you're not the only one madly in love…"

I can feel his heart beating faster and faster. Beating for me.

36361666R00068

Printed in Poland
by Amazon Fulfillment
Poland Sp. z o.o., Wrocław